Babar characters TM & © 1990 L. de Brunhoff
All rights reserved
Based on the animated series "Babar"
A Nelvana-Ellipse Presentation
a Nelvana Production in Association with The Clifford Ross Company, Ltd

**Based on characters created
by Jean and Laurent de Brunhoff**
Based on a story by J.D. Smith
Image adaptation by Van Gool-Lefèvre-Loiseaux
Produced by Twin Books U.K. Ltd, London

This 1990 edition published by JellyBean Press,
distributed by Outlet Book Company, Inc.,
a Random House Company,
225 Park Avenue South
New York NY 10003

ISBN 0-517-052083

8 7 6 5 4 3 2 1

Printed and bound in Barcelona, Spain by Cronion, S.A.

BABAR

The Race to the Moon

JellyBean Press
New York

One evening King Babar and Queen Celeste took the children to the theater in Celesteville. At the intermission, all the elephants in the audience strolled about the lobby, talking about the play.

"Papa," said Flora, "I think this must be the most beautiful place in the whole world."

"Look at that picture," said Pom to Alexander. "It's Papa when he was a little king. He looks just like me."

Babar overheard the children's remarks and they amused him. "Did you know," he said, "that the theater almost disappeared once? It was a long time ago." And he began the tale.

"One night . . .

. . . there was a terrible thunderstorm in Celesteville. A great bolt of lightning hit the theater and set it on fire. It burned all night, until it was only a shell."

The treasurer wanted to destroy what was left of the building, and the master builder wanted to construct a restaurant on the site. But Babar was determined to rebuild the theater, and he invited all the elephants to help.

Very soon, all one could hear was the sound of hammers, saws, and shovels. Every elephant came to lend a hand, including General Cornelius. Even Zephir and Celeste became useful workers.

"How wonderful," thought Babar, as the building grew. "The new theater will be even more beautiful than the old one." Then he asked, "By the way, has anyone seen Arthur? He's the only one missing."

Babar and Zephir went to look for their friend. "I only hope nothing has happened to him," said Babar. "Arthur always has such strange ideas. Oh, there he is! But what is that?"

"Over here," cried Arthur happily. "Come and see what I'm building. It's a million times better than an old theater."

"Oh no!" groaned Babar. "This time it's a rocket, and I know it will never fly."

Meanwhile, Basil, who was
spying for the rhinoceroses,
took a picture of the rocket.
Then he ran back to the palace
of Rataxes.

"Your Highness," he yelled, "Babar is planning to conquer the moon."

"By the horns on my nose!" trumpeted Rataxes. "*We* must be the first on the moon, not those great lummoxes. Basil, summon everyone. I want a rocket built within the hour. Get started."

Suddenly, a familiar call rang out: "Yoohoo! Rataxes, where are youuuu?"

"Good heavens, it's my wife," exclaimed Rataxes. Immediately, the dreaded rhino king became as gentle as a lamb. He left his throne and smiled weakly at Lady Rataxes.

"Now then, my little sweetums, have you forgotten our wedding anniversary?" screeched Lady Rataxes. "Where is my anniversary present?"

"Ah, yes, . . . present? . . . present?" The rhino king looked to the heavens for help, and had an idea. "The moon, my lovely one. I'm going to give you the moon."

"Oh Rataxes, you thoughtful thing," she cooed. "It's exactly what I wanted. My own moon."

A little later, a deafening roar rang in the skies over Celesteville. Spitting and smoking, a strange flying machine landed in front of the theater. A rhinoceros emerged from it and announced: "In the name of his Rhinexellence, Lord Rataxes, I claim this moon as the exclusive property of the rhinoceroses."

"This moon?" giggled Babar and his friends. "This isn't the moon. You've landed in the country of the elephants."

General Cornelius was not amused. "Rhinoceroses on the moon! Never! Babar, you must see that it would be unbearable!"

Arthur interrupted, "*We* must be the first to go. And I have a rocket."

"The whole idea is crazy!" said Babar. "Let's get back to rebuilding the theater." But everyone else disagreed. "No! No! I don't want to go to sleep by the light of a rhinoceros moon."

Poor Babar. Everyone had abandoned his special project. Instead, they wanted the moon.

The elephants had no time to lose.
Another rocket was ready to launch outside
Rataxes' palace.

Looking every inch a king, Rataxes waited to cut the cable attached to the rocket.

"Hurry, my darling," shrieked Madame Rataxes. "Get me that moon."

"Immediately, my dear," said Rataxes between his teeth. "Are the court photographers ready to capture the event of the century on film? Good! Here we go! 5, 4, 3, 2, 1 . . . *Blast off!*"

The engine throbbed, the fuses flamed, the heart of the jungle rocked with the vibration. At last, the rocket rose toward the sky. A great victory for the rhinoceroses! But suddenly, the pilot ejected and came drifting back to earth in his parachute. He had decided that the rocket could not fly properly because he was too heavy!

"Well, then," said Rataxes, "we must have a pilot who is lighter."

"I have an idea," whispered Basil.

In the land of the elephants, the choice of a pilot had been easier.

"We need a pilot who is light, agile, and clever," said Arthur. And someone else said, "That sounds just like Zephir."

Soon, Zephir was ready for his great adventure, dressed in a beautiful space suit. All the elephants came to see him off. Arthur announced, "My fabulous rocket is ready for launching." But Babar was worried.

27

And for good reason. Just as Zephir was climbing into the rocket, he was captured by the soldiers of Rataxes! They dragged him off like a sack of potatoes!

Babar went running after them, but he was too late.

"We can't let the rhinos send Zephir to the moon," said Babar. "Wait, I have it. Arthur, come with me. . . ."

Just as the rhinos were putting Zephir into the rocket, two scary figures appeared on the launch pad.

"Help! Martians!" stuttered Rataxes, who was trying to hide behind Basil.

"We are not Martians, you ignorant fool. We are Moonmen," said Babar and Arthur in disguise.

"Ah, yes, Moonmen. Uh, how can we help you?"

"If you do not wish to be turned into stew meat," said Babar, "leave the moon alone."

"But, Your Greatness, you see, my wife — she will never be content until . . ."

"Silence, miserable earthling," said Babar. "Give us your pilot. Then sign this treaty, and be quick about it."

"Yes, sign," whispered Basil to Rataxes. "We'll find some other way to send a rhinoceros to the moon."

When Babar, Arthur, and Zephir returned to Celesteville, the elephants were listening to a speech by Pompadour, the prime minister.

"Our beloved General Cornelius," said Pompadour, "has taken on the task of replacing our brave pilot, who was kidnapped. Courageously, he has . . ."

"Stop!" cried Babar. "Zephir is back, and Rataxes isn't going to the moon."

But it was too late. The rocket engines were already warming up.

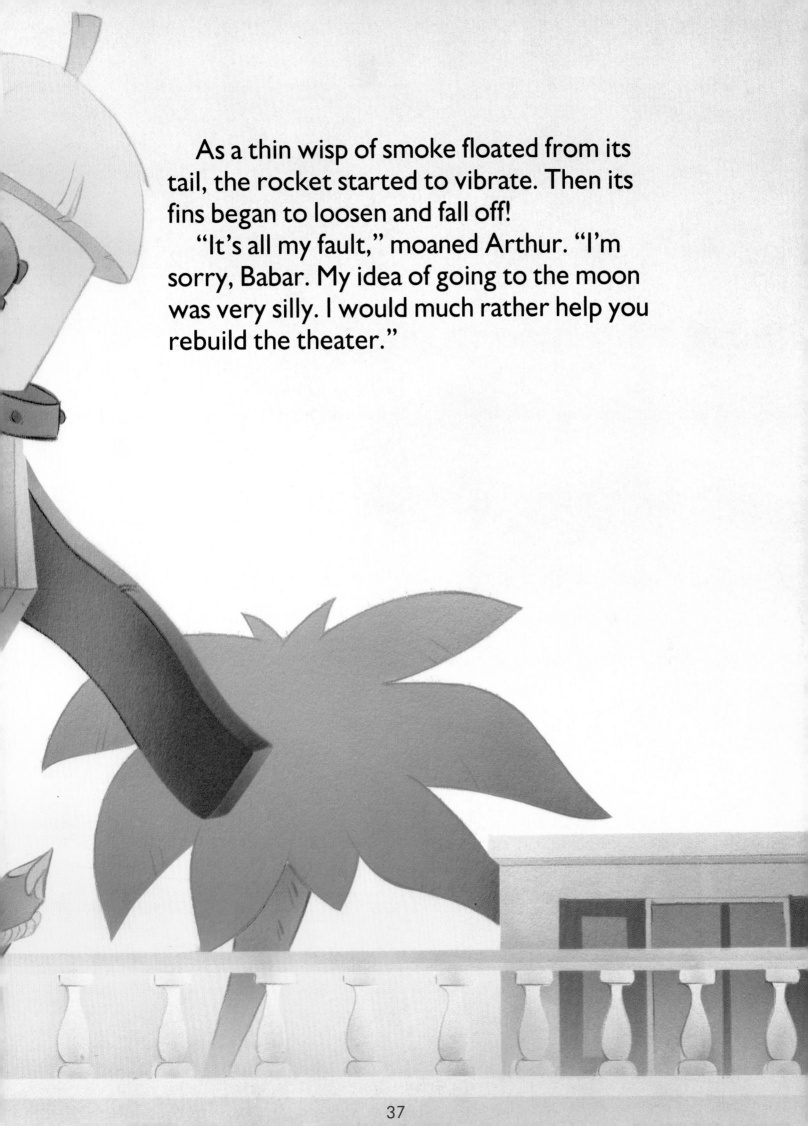

As a thin wisp of smoke floated from its tail, the rocket started to vibrate. Then its fins began to loosen and fall off!

"It's all my fault," moaned Arthur. "I'm sorry, Babar. My idea of going to the moon was very silly. I would much rather help you rebuild the theater."

Suddenly, the whole rocket began to shake. The engine dropped out and crushed one fin as flat as a pancake. Then, slowly, the rocket toppled over.

The elephants were shocked into silence. What about Cornelius? The old elephant was older than the oldest tree in the jungle. Even at his best, he trembled. His knees creaked at every step, and he couldn't see a foot in front of himself.

Quickly, Babar ran to find his old friend.

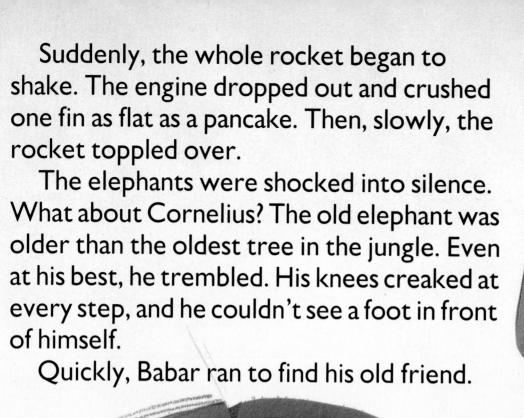
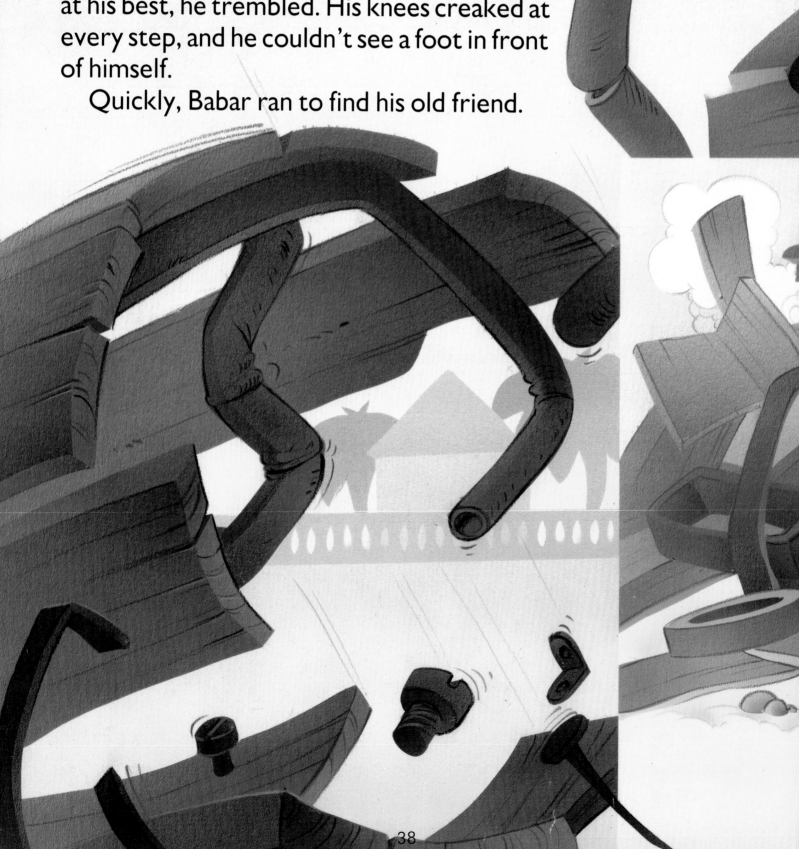

He pushed his way through the wreckage. At last! There was Cornelius, his ears trembling with emotion. But nothing was broken. Babar was so happy he hugged the old general

All Celesteville was relieved. The day after the accident, everyone returned to his work on the theater. The race to the moon was completely forgotten.

Zephir gladly gave up his position of astronaut. Celeste was back in her overalls. Even the elegant Pompadour was hammering away. And Babar couldn't have been happier. This time, he knew his theater would be rebuilt.

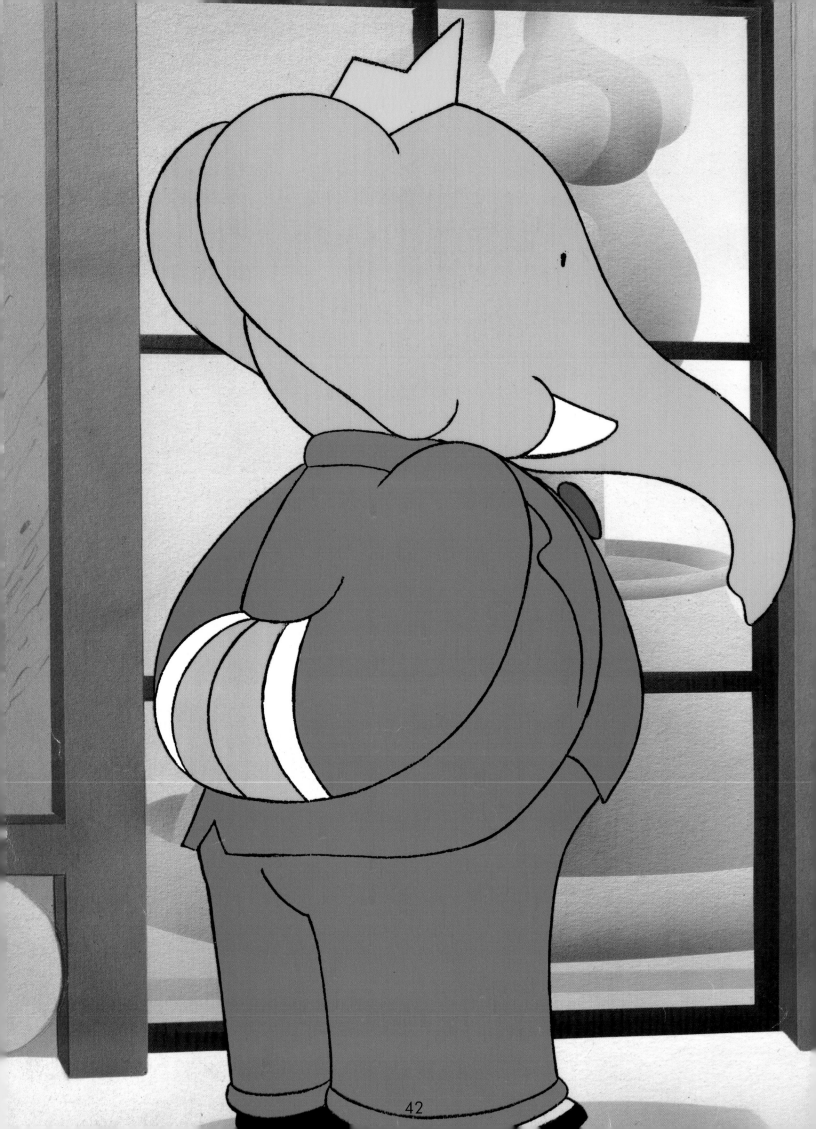

"And that, my dear children, is the story of the beautiful Celesteville theater," concluded Babar. "As soon as it was finished, we gave a series of incredible parties. Everyone in the jungle was invited. All the royal families arrived in silks and lace, surrounded by thousands of birds . . ."

"And Rataxes—did he come, too?" asked Alexander.

"Well, no. You see, the rhinoceroses could still think only of the moon."

43

"In fact, on moonlit nights, you could hear Rataxes and his wife arguing on their balcony."

"Rataxes, I want the moon to be full. I don't like these little crescent moons."

"But my dear, it's quite pretty that way."

"Also, I think I'd like it in another color. And maybe it would look better over there."

"But, my dear . . ."

Those two never stopped squabbling.